The
Slithery Shakedown

by

Tracey Hecht

Illustrations by
Josie Yee

Fabled Films Press
New York

Chapter 1

The moon was high.

The sun had set.

Nighttime had arrived.

But Bismark's friends had not.

"They're late!"
Bismark said to the darkness.

Bismark tapped his foot.

Bismark put his fists
to his hips.

Bismark scrunched
his tiny pink nose.

This sugar glider was peeved!

"We sugar gliders are always on time," Bismark said.

He smoothed the fur on his chest.

He admired his fluffy tail.

He stretched his stretchy wings.

Suddenly, the grasses swooshed.

Bismark jumped!

A nose popped from the tall reeds.

The nose was long.

The nose was smooth.

The nose belonged to a pangolin.

Chapter 2

The pangolin was named Tobin.

Tobin was Bismark's friend.

Bismark relaxed.

Tobin blinked his little black eyes.

Tobin stretched his short neck.

Tobin scratched
his scaly rump.

Tobin had just woken up.
He was nocturnal,
awake by night, asleep by day.

Just then,

the grasses **swooshed** again.

This time a red fox stepped from the
tall reeds.

Her fur was soft.

Her ears were pointy.

Her name was Dawn.

"Amigos!" Bismark sang out.

"We are all here! The Nocturnal Brigade."

Bismark hopped on a rock.

"I shall lead us on an adventure!"
Bismark said to his friends.

"I am Bismark the Brave."

Bismark stood tall.

Bismark squatted small.

Bismark puffed out his chest.

Tobin giggled.

Dawn's mouth curved in a
gentle smile.

They were used to their silly friend.

Dawn rose from her haunches.

"We have been asleep all day," Dawn said.

"Why don't we start our adventure with
some breakfast?"

But as Dawn spoke, something behind

Bismark caught her eye.

It was blue.

It was shimmery.

It made a noise like 'sssssssss'.

It was a snake!

Chapter 3

"Did sss-someone sss-say breakfassst?"
the snake said.

Bismark spun around.

Behind him was a long, blue, shimmery snake.

The snake slid from the grass.

The snake raised its head.

The snake flicked its flickery tongue.

"Bismark, look out!" Dawn cried.

Bismark froze.

The snake slithered closer.

"Sss-scrumptious!" the snake said.

"A sss-scrawny, little sss-sugar glider.

The perfect sss-snack!"

Bismark screamed.

"Save me!" Bismark cried.

"That snake will turn me into a sugar glider stew!"

Bismark scurried behind Dawn.

Dawn narrowed her eyes.

Dawn took a step forward.

"Stop!" Dawn told the snake.

"This sugar glider is not your snack!"

The snake swished its tail.

"Sss-says who?" the snake replied.

"Says me," Dawn shot back.

Tobin looked at his small sugar glider friend.

Tobin summoned his courage.

"And me!" Tobin said.

"Sí!" Bismark shouted.

"Says she! And he!"
 Bismark pointed to his friends.

"Oh, and me!" Bismark said.

The snake stared at the fox.

The fox stared at the snake.

The sugar glider and the
pangolin stared, too.

This was a standoff.

Chapter 4

The snake gave a sly smile.

The snake stretched very tall.

"Try and sss-stop me," the snake said.

"Certainly!" Dawn replied.

"Sure thing," Tobin added.

"Seriously?" Bismark bawled.

The snake got ready to spring.

Dawn snarled.

"Slither back where you came from!"
Dawn told the snake.

Tobin raised a sharp, taloned claw.

"Take off!" Tobin told the snake.

Bismark took a deep breath.

"Yeah, bb-beat it, you bb-bully!"
Bismark sputtered.

The snake studied the three friends.

One tall. One small. One medium.

But together, tough stuff.

The snake sputtered.

"On sss-second thought," the snake said,
"it might be time for me to sss-skedaddle!

SSS-Sayonara!"

And the snake slithered back
into the woods.

Chapter 5

"By the stars!" Bismark cried.

"We scared that bully away!

Bb-bravo!"

Bismark was shaking.

"Bismark, were you afraid?"
Tobin asked his friend.

"Nn-no," Bismark said.
"I was nn-not afraid. I am bb-brave."

"Bismark," Dawn said. "Everyone gets afraid."

'Oh goodness, that's true!" Tobin said.

"I was scared of that snake."

"I was also scared," Dawn said.

"You can be scared and brave, too."

"Bb-but I am Bismark!" Bismark said.

"Sugar glider spec-tac-u-lar!

Strong, spunky, and never ss-scared!"

Tobin smiled.

Dawn raised an eyebrow.

But Bismark gasped!

Something blue and shimmery
had caught his eye.

Chapter 6

Bismark blinked.

Bismark tried to be brave.

Bismark bent low to see.

The thing was blue.

The thing was shimmery.

But the thing was not slithery.

"By the moon!" Bismark said.

"Look here! That snake slithered right out of its skin."

Bismark reached for the snakeskin.

He held it up high.

He tore off a piece.

He tied it around his neck.

"I am brave," Bismark declared.

Bismark gave a piece to Tobin.

"Oh goodness!" Tobin said.

Tobin twirled in his new, blue cape.

Bismark gave a piece to Dawn.

"Very nice," Dawn said.

Dawn admired her new, shimmery shawl.

"The perfect uniform for our perfect brigade," Dawn said.

"The Nocturnal Brigade!" Tobin cheered.

Bismark smiled. "Bold in adventure.

And best of all,

brave!"

The NOCTURNALS

Look for The Next Adventure!

Join The Nocturnal Brigade at nocturnalsworld.com for updates!

The NoCTURNALS

FUN FACTS!

What are The Nocturnal Animals?

Pangolin: The pangolin is covered with keratin scales on most of its body except its belly and face. Pangolins spray a stinky odor, much like a skunk, to ward off danger. It then curls into a ball to protect against attack. Pangolins have long, sticky tongues to eat ants and termites. Pangolins do not have teeth.

Red Fox: The red fox has reddish fur with a big bushy tail and a white tip. Red foxes are clever creatures with keen eyesight. They have large, upright ears to hear sounds far away.

Sugar Glider: The sugar glider is a small marsupial. It looks like a flying squirrel. It has short gray fur and black rings around its big eyes. It has a black stripe that runs from its nose to the end of its tail. Sugar gliders have special skin that stretches from the ankle to the wrist. This special skin allows sugar gliders to glide from tree to tree to find food and escape danger.

Blue Bellied Snake: Blue bellied snakes are naturally shy and won't bite unless they're threatened. They shed their skin in one piece to allow for further growth. Snakes smell with their tongues and have tiny fibers on their tongues that help them distinguish scents. They don't chew their food, but swallow it whole.

Nighttime Fun Facts!

Nocturnal animals are animals that are awake and active at night. They sleep during the day.

Pomelos are fruits much like grapefruits. They are the Nocturnal Brigade's favorite food to eat. They have yellow or light green peels and pink citrusy flesh. They are the biggest citrus fruits in the world!

Grow & Read Storytime Activities
For The Nocturnals Early Reader Books!

Download Free Printables:

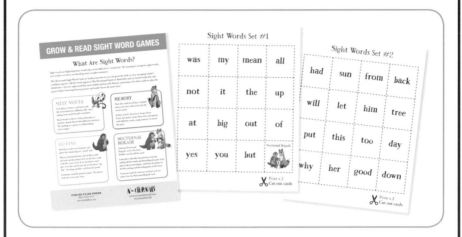

Sight Word Games

Brigade Mask Craft and Coloring Pages!

Visit **nocturnalsworld.com**
#NocturnalsWorld

About the Author

Tracey Hecht is a writer and entrepreneur who has written, directed and produced for film. She created a Nocturnals Read Aloud Writing Program in partnership with the New York Public Library that has expanded nationwide. Tracey splits her time between Oquossoc, Maine and New York City.

About the Illustrator

Josie Yee is an award-winning illustrator and graphic artist specializing in children's publishing. She received her BFA from Arizona State University and studied Illustration at the Academy of Art University in San Francisco. She lives in New York City with her daughter, Ana, and their cat, Dude.

About Fabled Films & Fabled Films Press

Fabled Films is a publishing and entertainment company creating original content for young readers and middle grade audiences. Fabled Films Press combines strong literary properties with high quality production values to connect books with generations of parents and their children. Each property is supported by websites, educator guides and activities for bookstores, educators and librarians, as well as videos, social media content and supplemental entertainment for additional platforms.

fabledfilms.com

FABLED FILMS PRESS
NEW YORK CITY

Read All of The Grow & Read Nocturnal Brigade Adventures!

This series can help children enjoy learning to read and is perfect for shared reading and reading aloud.

Great For Kids Ages 5-7

Level 1

Level 2

Level 3

All titles are available as eBooks.
Visit nocturnalsworld.com to download fun nighttime activities
#NocturnalsWorld